The Hulk
Fights Back

UNIVERSAL PICTURES PRESENTS IN ASSOCIATION WITH MARVEL ENTERPRISES A VALHALLA MOTION PICTURES / GOOD MACHINE PRODUCTION AN ANG LEE FILM "THE HULK" ERIC BANA JENNIFER CONNELLY SAM ELLIOTT JOSH LUCAS AND NICK NOLTE MUSIC BY MYCHAEL DANNA COSTUME DESIGNER MARIT ALLEN EDITOR TIM SQUYRES ACE PRODUCTION DESIGNER RICK HEINRICHS DIRECTOR OF PHOTOGRAPHY FREDERICK ELMES ASC EXECUTIVE PRODUCERS STAN LEE KEVIN FEIGE PRODUCED BY GALE ANNE HURD AVI ARAD JAMES SCHAMUS LARRY FRANCO WRITTEN BY JAMES SCHAMUS DIRECTED BY ANG LEE

MARVEL THIS FILM IS NOT YET RATED   SPECIAL VISUAL EFFECTS AND ANIMATION BY INDUSTRIAL LIGHT & MAGIC   www.thehulk.com   A UNIVERSAL PICTURE UNIVERSAL

THE HULK AND RELATED COMIC BOOK CHARACTERS ™ & © 2002 MARVEL CHARACTERS, INC.   © 2003 UNIVERSAL STUDIOS

The Hulk™: The Hulk Fights Back

First published in the USA by HarperCollins Publishers Inc. in 2003
First published in Great Britain by HarperCollinsEntertainment in 2003

HarperCollinsEntertainment is an imprint of HarperCollinsPublishers Ltd,
77 - 85 Fulham Palace Road, Hammersmith, London W6 8JB

The HarperCollins website address is
www.**fire**and**water**.com

1 3 5 7 9 10 8 6 4 2

ISBN 0-00-716244-8
Colour reproductions by Dot Gradations Ltd, UK
Printed and bound by Printing Express Ltd., Hong Kong

www.thehulk.com

The Hulk
Fights Back

Adapted by Jasmine Jones
Based on the motion picture screenplay
by James Schamus

HarperCollins*Entertainment*
An Imprint of HarperCollins*Publishers*

Chapter 1

On the Run

The Hulk sped across the desert, his enormous feet thudding over the hot sand. His green skin glistened with a light film of sweat, but the Hulk wasn't tired. He didn't even feel the heat of the sun beating down over his back as he ran on and on. The Hulk had only one thought—he had to get to San Francisco. He had to find Betty Ross, his only friend.

The Hulk had not always been a huge, hideous monster with rippling muscles and green skin. Only a few days ago, he had been a mild-mannered research scientist named Bruce Krenzler. But there had always been something strange about Bruce. Even as a child, whenever he got angry, his muscles would bulge and shake uncontrollably. He had only recently discovered his past—Bruce's real last name is Banner. His father, David, killed Bruce's mother. Bruce was then adopted and raised by the Krenzlers.

Bruce also discovered the source of his illness. David Banner had also been a scientist. He had performed experiments on himself, and those experiments

affected his son's blood before Bruce was even born. As a child, Bruce learned to deal with his anger by keeping a tight rein on it, making sure that it never got out of control.

That had worked well—for a while. Then one day Bruce was exposed to gamma radiation in his laboratory. He had been trying to protect his coworkers, Betty and Harper, from an accident. When Bruce saw that the system designed to contain the radiation had failed, he threw his body between his friends and the deadly beams. That radiation unleashed the monster within him. Now, whenever Bruce is angry, his muscles expand until he changes into the Hulk. And when the Hulk becomes angrier, he grows even larger and more ferocious.

Betty had tried to help the Hulk. She had called her father, who was a general in the army, and asked him to take the Hulk somewhere safe. Betty wanted to figure out how to turn him back into Bruce Banner—permanently. General Ross knew that the Hulk was dangerous, so he agreed to help. The General had known Bruce's father many years before, and had made sure that David Banner went to jail for the illegal experiments he had been performing. With the help of the U.S. Army, General Ross transported Bruce to a top secret research facility in the desert. Unfortunately, Glen Talbot, Bruce's rival, was also at the facility. He wanted to study the Hulk. Talbot provoked Bruce until the Hulk was unleashed, and then the Hulk escaped from his captors.

The Hulk has been on the run since then.

The air was silent all around him as the Hulk

raced farther and farther into the desert. His heart pounded in his ears as the rugged landscape flew by. Suddenly, the Hulk heard a mechanical buzzing as four helicopters pursued him. The Hulk had known that General Ross would come after him, but he didn't slow down or change direction—he simply charged ahead.

"Be advised," General Ross told the helicopter pilots, "the subject is moving very fast out there." The general was on board a Black Hawk helicopter, looking down at the fleeing Hulk. The Hulk took a running leap—an incredible jump—and kept going. "The terrain doesn't seem to be an obstacle," the General added tensely. He was concerned about what the Hulk might do if he wasn't caught quickly. General Ross had already warned the President of the United States that he may have to take extreme measures to stop the Hulk.

"Roger," one of the pilots said, signaling that he had understood.

The other pilot said that he was ready to fire at the Hulk.

"You are cleared to attack," General Ross said.

The Hulk had reached a steep cliff. With a mighty leap, he jumped to the top of the rocks and looked out over the landscape. For a moment, everything was silent.

Suddenly four black military helicopters rose up

before him from the valley below. They hovered above, ready to fire.

The Hulk reacted quickly. He reached out and grabbed a propeller of the closest helicopter. The propeller was in motion, so when the Hulk held it, the helicopter swayed and slammed into him. The Hulk wrestled with the helicopter tail, struggling to force it to the ground. Evenly matched, the helicopter and the Hulk rolled down the side of the cliff.

The other three helicopters ducked and buzzed as they struggled to regroup around the Hulk, who had instantly picked himself up from his fall and started climbing. The Hulk moved quickly, darting from cliff to ravine, charging easily across immense obstacles.

"Combat spread!" one of the pilots ordered. The helicopters moved into position.

"I do not want him to move any farther west," General Ross warned.

The Hulk continued to climb, scaling up a canyon wall. There was a thunderous noise as the helicopters fired at him, but the Hulk didn't get hurt. Bullets couldn't penetrate the Hulk's skin—nothing could. He climbed to the top of the ledge and hauled himself over the edge. Just then, one of the helicopters fired a missile at the ledge. The Hulk let out a roar as the ground disappeared beneath his feet. Chunks of rock rained down into the desert valley below as the Hulk tumbled down the side of the rock face.

But even that wasn't enough to stop the Hulk. He picked himself up and leaped out of the rubble. The Hulk flew high into the air—right over General Ross's helicopter!

"He's headed straight for San Francisco," General Ross realized as the Hulk leaped again.

The air was calm, and the Hulk felt a moment of peace as his huge body tore through the clouds high in the sky. Then gravity pulled him back down to earth. The ground shook as the Hulk landed, then he crouched and leaped again. Nothing could stop him now.

Chapter 2

The Chase

Betty Ross stood watching the military police lead away Bruce's father, David Banner. He didn't seem the slightest bit worried that he was being hauled into a jail cell on a military base. The truth was, David Banner—or the Father, as he was sometimes called—wasn't worried. That was because the Father had a secret: he could absorb power from any object. If he touched a rock, he could become as hard as a stone. If he touched a knife, he could become as sharp as a blade. The Father knew that with this power no prison could hold him for long. But nobody else knew that.

Betty's cell phone chirped and she flipped it open. "Yes?" she said.

"Betty," General Ross said, "he—it—got out."

Betty swallowed hard. She knew her father was talking about the Hulk.

"He's headed toward San Francisco, probably to you," General Ross added. "Get to the base—"

"I'm already there," Betty interrupted. "And his father—he's turned himself in."

"His father!" General Ross cried. "I'll order up a security detail. Stay there."

Betty folded up her phone and looked out the window at the San Francisco Bay. The Golden Gate Bridge seemed to glow in the brilliant sunshine. But Betty knew that terrible danger lay behind the peaceful scene . . . and that it was drawing closer.

* * *

The Hulk had reached the Sierra Nevadas, and he was still on the move. He wasn't alone, though. Three F-22 Raptor jets were right behind him.

"Check fire," General Ross told them. "The area's too populated. We've got to try to get him out to sea."

An operator's voice sounded over the general's earphones. "The mayor's on the line," she said.

"General," the mayor of San Francisco said, "I'm bringing out the welcome committee for whatever it is you're sending me." A siren sounded in the background. The mayor had just put all emergency vehicles and special police forces on high alert.

"Thank you, Mr. Mayor," General Ross said. "I'm hoping our stay will be a brief one." General Ross knew that the sooner he could catch the Hulk, the less damage the monster would do. He only hoped they could capture him quickly.

Chapter 3

City by the Bay

The Hulk stood atop the Marin Headlands, overlooking the Golden Gate Bridge. The city was just across the water; he had almost reached San Francisco. The Raptor jets buzzed overhead.

With one giant leap, the Hulk jumped toward the Golden Gate Bridge, landing on one of the arches. Below him, cars on the bridge honked and screeched to a stop. The jets circled back to take a pass at the Hulk. But one of them was flying too low—it was about to slam into a helicopter!

The jet pilot swerved to avoid hitting the helicopter, but now he was headed straight for the bridge. The Hulk saw what was happening—he had to do something! With lightning speed, the Hulk jumped onto the jet. It dipped and swooped under his weight. The Hulk bent over, clinging tightly to the jet as it passed beneath the bridge. His solid back scraped along the underside of the bridge, sending a crease through it, but the bridge remained intact. Nobody was hurt.

"Okay, you've got him!" General Ross cried out. "Now take him on a ride to the top of the world. Let's see what some thin air will do to him."

The pilot flew his jet straight up into the sky. The Hulk didn't let go as the plane soared through the clouds. But high in the sky, there wasn't much oxygen to breathe, and the air was very cold. The pilot had a special oxygen tank in the jet, but the Hulk didn't have one. He began to lose consciousness. When the pilot saw that the Hulk was getting sleepy, he tipped the plane back toward earth, and the Hulk slid off the end.

The Hulk was falling, falling. . . .

Chapter 4

Damage Control

With a shattering boom, the Hulk splashed into San Francisco Bay. He plunged straight to the bottom with so much force that half his body got stuck in the muddy floor. Awake now and trapped underwater, the Hulk struggled to escape.

General Ross's helicopter flew over the bay. The water was rough and choppy. There was no sign of the Hulk.

Suddenly the surface of the water churned, sending off mountains of foam as the Hulk came up for air.

The jets and helicopters took aim at the Hulk, but he was too quick for them. In a flash, he dove back into the bay. Spotting some underwater drains, the Hulk thought fast and swam into one of them. Now he was on his way into the city.

"We are going to cause a lot of damage if we start shooting into downtown San Francisco," one of the pilots warned General Ross.

"You are cleared to fire," General Ross replied. "Let me worry about the damage." His mouth was set in a grim line. The truth was, the general *was* worried. But he knew the Hulk had to be stopped, no matter the cost.

A few minutes later, General Ross's helicopter set down at the military base. Betty Ross ran out to meet her father.

"Betty," General Ross said sadly, "I don't know what choice I have. I must destroy him."

"You can't!" Betty cried, shouting to be heard over the noise of the helicopter. "Enraging him just makes him stronger. And you'll destroy San Francisco in the process. There's only one way to stop him," she said, her eyes pleading. "Give him some breathing room."

Chapter 5

The Man Inside the Beast

Ding! Ding!

The conductor rang the bell of the cable car as it made its way toward Market Street in downtown San Francisco. No one noticed a small crack in the street behind the trolley until the crack grew bigger and bigger; then the road began tilting upward.

A passerby saw what was happening and jumped out of the way of the spreading crack just as a water main burst. Caps flew off nearby fire hydrants, and plumes of water exploded into the air.

The Hulk was in the sewer lines, beneath the streets of San Francisco. With each step he took, he pushed up against the ceiling of pipes overhead, cracking the sidewalk above him. Finally he came to a manhole. The Hulk poked his head out from beneath the cover, squinting in the daylight. He was on a hill, the street sloping below him. People all around panicked as the Hulk climbed out of the sewer.

A few police officers saw the Hulk and came running at him, weapons drawn. Overhead, a fleet of

Apache helicopters approached, ready to take aim. Feeling trapped, the Hulk let out a terrifying roar. People screamed and ran away, but the military forces kept coming toward him. Hundreds of soldiers encircled him, on the ground and even on the tops of surrounding buildings. They paused, ready to strike.

No one moved.

Suddenly the Hulk heard footsteps behind him. When he turned, he saw Betty walking toward him.

"All units," General Ross commanded, "hold your fire."

When the Hulk saw Betty, he dropped to his knees. He let out a cry that was full of shame . . . and pain. He had never meant to cause so much destruction and fear—but when the anger overtook him, he couldn't stop himself. Could his friend ever forgive him?

Betty caught her breath. She could see that Bruce was trapped inside the Hulk. She knew she had to help him. Betty stepped closer.

The Hulk winced and turned away, but Betty reached out and touched his face. Suddenly the Hulk's body began to shrink. Sweat poured from his skin as the Hulk became smaller and smaller, until he was Bruce Banner once again.

Bruce smiled weakly at Betty. "You found me," he whispered.

Betty glanced around at the crowd gathered nearby. "You weren't that hard to find," she said.

Bruce looked at her closely. "Yes," he said, "I was." He meant she had found him, Bruce, buried deep within the Hulk and beneath all of that terrifying anger. It had taken a special kind of courage for Betty to do what she had done.

A tear trickled down Betty's cheek, but she didn't say a word.

"Hey," Bruce said gently, "I'm just grateful we got the chance . . . to say—" his voice deepened, choked with emotion—"good-bye." Bruce knew the military would take him to prison, and they would never let the Hulk live.

Betty drew Bruce into a long hug. She was afraid to let him go.

Chapter 6

Like Father, Like Son?

Bruce Banner sat on a chair at the end of a large airplane hangar on a military base. The structure was bare, lit with harsh lights. Electromagnetic weapons were trained on Bruce, ready to turn him to ashes if he changed into the Hulk again. Bruce hung his head in distress. He knew that this was the end—the Hulk had to be destroyed . . . forever.

Betty's gray eyes were serious and her heart ached as she stood with her father and a few others, watching Bruce on a video monitor.

"Here's the deal," General Ross announced, "he stays on the base here until we get final word from C-Three on how to dispose of him. The slightest hint he's putting on weight, or if he curls his lip a little too meanly, or he starts looking like an avocado—we turn up the juice and he's incinerated immediately." He turned to his daughter. "Betty, you'd best prepare yourself for the orders we're going to get," he added in a gentle voice.

Betty nodded, blinking to hide her tears.

"We've established a two-hundred-yard perimeter, sir," a colonel reported. "If we deploy the electromagnetic array, there should be no collateral damage." That meant when they fired at the Hulk, no one would be hurt—except for the Hulk, of course.

"It'll be quite a show, though," General Ross said grimly.

Just then, a transport truck pulled up. Guards jumped down, and one of them yanked open the door in the back to reveal David Banner. The Father was bound with chains at his hands and feet. The troops led him toward the end of the hangar, where his son sat waiting. The Father didn't say anything as he passed General Ross and Betty.

When Bruce saw his father's stooped figure walking toward him, he stood up, squinting into the bright lights. David Banner shuffled forward until he and his son were face to face. The Father hung his head.

"I should have killed you," Bruce whispered. He thought about the damage this man, his father, had done. The Father had killed Bruce's mother and turned Bruce into a monster.

"As I should have killed *you*," the Father replied. He lifted his eyes to meet his son's.

"I wish you had," Bruce said, his voice quiet. He sank down onto the chair and buried his head in his hands. "I saw her last night," he said finally. He was

talking about his mother. Bruce had thought that he had no memories of her. "In my mind's eye, I saw her face," he went on. "Brown hair, brown eyes. She smiled at me, she leaned down and kissed my cheek. I can almost remember a smell, like—" Bruce thought for a moment—"like desert flowers."

The Father nodded. "Her favorite perfume."

"My mother." Bruce swallowed hard. "I don't even know her name." He sighed, and a tear snaked down his face.

The Father walked over to one of the nearby lamps. "That's good," he said quietly. "Crying will do you good." The Father smiled absently, remembering his absorbing power. He was certain he could become electrifying, with the help of a lamp cord. And who knew what else he could absorb? Suddenly he dropped the cord and walked toward his son, his arms outstretched.

Bruce's head snapped up. "No," he said tensely, eyeing his father's chained hands. "Please don't touch me." He looked closely at David Banner, and his voice softened. "Maybe, once, you were my father. But you're not now—you never will be."

The Father looked at his son. "Is that so?" he asked. "Well, I have news for you. I didn't come here to see you." David Banner's eyes glinted dangerously. "I came for my son."

Bruce's dark eyebrows drew together in confusion.

"My *real* son," the Father went on, his voice a low hiss. "The one inside of you. You are merely a superficial shell surrounding him, ready to be torn off at a moment's notice."

"Think whatever you like," Bruce said uneasily. "I don't care. Just go now."

"But Bruce," the Father protested, "I have found a cure, for me." His eyes narrowed, and his voice lowered to a threatening growl. "You see, my cells can transform too. They can absorb enormous amounts of energy. But, unlike your cells, mine are unstable," he explained. "I gave you life, now you must give it back to me. Only I'll be a million times more powerful."

"Stop," Bruce commanded, shifting away from his father.

"Think of it," the Father said, jerking his head toward the hangar door that led to the military base outside, "all those men out there, in their uniforms, barking and swallowing orders. Think of all the harm they've done to you, to me. And now we can make them and their governments disappear in a flash. Your power," he whispered, eyes glittering, "in me."

Bruce's eyes widened in horror. "I'd rather die," he said.

"And indeed you shall," the Father replied evenly. "And be reborn a hero."

Bruce lunged toward his father. "Go!" he screamed.

"Stop your bawling, you weak little speck of human debris," the Father snarled. "I'll go." Suddenly he turned and grabbed one of the thick snakes of electrical cord at his feet. In a flash he tore it apart. "Just watch me go!" the Father shouted, laughing wildly. The wires sparked and sputtered for a moment before David Banner shoved them into his mouth. Above, the lights in the hangar dimmed.

"No!" Bruce shouted, jumping at his father, but the electricity rolling off David Banner threw Bruce backward.

Seeing the emergency, General Ross gave the order to fire the electromagnetic weapons. Energy surged through the room . . . and into the out-stretched arms of the Father. Lights went out across San Francisco as David Banner absorbed all the power in the city! His body seemed to glow as energy coursed through him. The chains that held his hands and feet crackled, then fell away. The Father flung out his arms, sending out an electromagnetic field. The hangar sizzled with electricity.

"Hit them again!" General Ross commanded.

"We can't, sir," a soldier informed him. "There's no power."

"Then move in there," the General barked, "with everything you've got. Fire at will."

The Father laughed, ignoring the soldiers on the move around him. He glanced in the direction Bruce

had been thrown by the electrical current, looking for his son.

Slam!

A huge green fist blasted the Father through the roof of the hangar and across the bay. With a horrifying roar, the Hulk leaped after the Father.

The earth trembled as father and son landed at the edge of a tranquil lake on a distant mountain. A firestorm of electricity surrounded them as they staggered to their feet. As they faced each other, the Hulk realized that the Father was almost as tall as he was. But the electricity seemed to have drained from him.

The Father laughed madly. "You see," he said, "nothing can stop me, son. I absorb it all, and give it back."

The Hulk roared in reply and swung at his father, pounding him mercilessly with one fist, then the other. The Father took each blow calmly. With each hit, he seemed to grow bigger . . . and greener. He was absorbing the Hulk's energy.

After a moment the Hulk stepped back, realizing the horrible truth. The Father was as large as he was.

"Go on, son," the Father taunted. "The more you fight me, the more of you I become."

The Hulk hesitated, confused. How could he win this fight? His mind reeled as he looked around for something—anything he could use against David

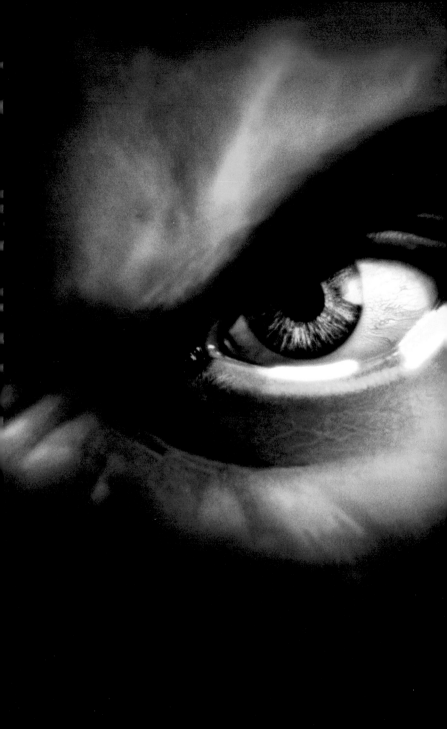

Banner. Suddenly the Hulk's eyes fell on a large boulder. He hauled it up onto his shoulder and hurled it at the Father.

The rock crashed down on the Father, who immediately absorbed its energy and turned to stone. The Hulk picked up the rock and dropped it again, slamming it over and over into the Father. The Father began to break up, smashing apart until he was little more than a pile of rubble. With a final mighty blow, the Hulk hurled the boulder down onto the mountain of rocks, sending chips of stone and clouds of rock dust flying.

For a moment, it seemed as though the Father had been defeated. But as the Hulk brushed away the stone fragments and dust that had landed on him, he managed to transfer energy to his father's broken form. It wasn't much, but it was enough for the Father's body to rebuild itself.

Furious, the Hulk lashed out at his father with his fists. But that was a mistake—David Banner only grew more powerful as he absorbed each blow. He lunged at his son. With every strike, the two staggered closer to the lake. The air around them grew colder, and the water in the lake began to turn icy as the two stumbled into the water.

Back at the base, an officer was reading satellite images, trying to locate the Hulk. General Ross and Betty peered at the monitors overhead. Finally, the officer locked on to the correct location and zoomed in. "We're reading a phenomenal drop in temperatures," he reported, "but simultaneous radio-logical activity."

"The ambient energy," Betty said, referring to the energy in the air and the ground around the Father and the Hulk. "They're absorbing it all."

General Ross sent fighter jets after the Hulk and the Father. They screamed through the air on their way to the mountain lake.

Chapter 7

An Explosive End

The Father and the Hulk were locked in a death grip as water began to freeze around them. The Hulk was growing colder, but he knew he had to keep fighting. He couldn't let his father win.

The Hulk's mind reached back into the past—back when he was the child Bruce Banner. In his memory it was Christmas, and he was playing with the floppy dolls his father had given him. His father was playing too.

"This one can fly," young Bruce said, laughing. "He's faster."

"But mine will eat yours right up," the Father said.

"No!" Bruce said. "He won't. Mine is flying away."

The Father smiled. "Yes," he said. "You're flying away."

Snapping back to reality, the Hulk realized how the Father planned to win. He wanted to harness the Hulk's rage. But the Hulk couldn't let that happen. He knew that the only way to stop his father was to

take the rage away from himself. Bruce had to forgive his father. And then his father could have the son he had come for.

Take him, Bruce Banner thought as the ice around him began to crack. *He's yours.* The Hulk went limp in the Father's grip.

With an evil grin, the Father held the Hulk's fist into his stomach. The Hulk struggled as his strength flowed into his father.

"Come to me," the Father said, "my son."

The Hulk grew smaller and smaller. Finally, the body of Bruce Banner fell from his father's giant grip and splashed into the icy lake. He sank slowly to the bottom.

Now the Father was enormous, towering above the mountains. Looking over the horizon, he caught a glimpse of the puny fighter jets that were on their way toward him. He laughed, and the earth shook with the noise, louder than thunder. The Father's earsplitting laughter went on and on . . . and then stopped. He looked down at his stomach, which was swirling with wild electricity. His body was growing larger and larger—it wouldn't stop!

The Father thrashed wildly, looking for his son, but the Hulk was nowhere in sight. "You!" the Father howled. "The reaction! You tricked me! Take it back! It's not stopping!"

General Ross watched what was happening on a

television monitor back at the military base. "Gentlemen," he commanded, "release." At that moment, one of the jets unleashed an enormous bomb. The Father was screaming in agony, still growing wildly with the energy he had absorbed from the Hulk, when the bomb slammed into him.

A brilliant orange cloud filled the sky as the Father exploded in a massive flare of energy.

General Ross watched the explosion on the monitor. He dropped his face into his hands.

"It's okay," Betty whispered, putting a hand on his shoulder. She looked up at the screen, where the sky was still. The Father was gone . . . forever. And Bruce's body lay at the bottom of the frigid mountain lake.

Betty knew that she would never see Bruce again.

Epilogue

In the Thick, Green Jungle

Months later, Betty was sitting in her new laboratory, looking at strands of DNA through a microscope, when the phone rang. She picked up the receiver absentmindedly and held it to her ear.

"Betty?" barked her father's voice. "That you?"

"Hi, Dad," Betty said with a sigh. She adjusted her microscope slightly.

"I'm glad I caught you," General Ross said.

"I'm glad you called," Betty replied.

"Betty," the general began, "you and I, we both know, of course, that Banner . . . well, he couldn't have survived that, that explosion and all. . . ."

Betty turned away from the microscope, listening intently. There was a strange note in her father's voice. "Dad, what's up?" she asked.

"You know," General Ross said with an uneasy laugh, "the usual loonies, thinking they've spotted big green guys . . . "

"They have," Betty joked, "on the side of their frozen vegetable packages."

"I know this goes without saying," General Ross went on, "but if—and I say *if*—by any chance he should contact you, try to get in touch . . . Well, you'd tell me now, wouldn't you?"

"No," Betty said slowly, "I wouldn't." She bit her lip, hesitating. "You know as well as I do I wouldn't have to. My phones are bugged, my house is under surveillance, my computers are tapped. So contacting me is the last thing I'd ever want Bruce to do, because—" Betty's voice was thick with emotion, but she forced herself to go on, "because I love him, I always will. And I pray to God every night and every morning he never tries to see me again for the rest of my life."

There was silence at the other end of the line. "I'm sorry, Betty," her father said finally. "I am so sorry."

"I know you are, Dad," Betty whispered into the receiver. "I know."

* * *

A short time later, in a jungle in Central America, three relief workers were tending to a few families. The families were poor, and some of the children were sick. It had just stopped pouring and the air was thick with humidity. The people had trekked through the rain to the aid tent for supplies and medicine.

A farmer entered the tent with his eight-year-old son. He held out the boy to one of the volunteers, a man with dark hair and a dark beard. None of the people the man worked with knew his real name was Bruce Banner. He had given them a false name when he applied for the job. He knew it would take him far away from San Francisco and from his past as the Hulk.

Bruce inspected the boy carefully, and noted that he looked glassy-eyed and feverish. "You need to give him this three times a day for ten days," Bruce told the farmer in Spanish, reaching for some medicine. "Okay?" He turned to the little boy. "You listen to your father when he tells you to take this medicine, okay?"

The boy nodded weakly. *"Sí,"* he said. The boy looked up at his father and smiled, and his father smiled back.

Just then, a group of men strode out of the jungle. They were wearing camouflage and carrying guns. Bruce knew what they were the minute he saw them—guerillas. They walked into the tent and began stealing supplies.

"We need these medicines for the people who live here," Bruce told them.

"Who are you to say what is needed, foreigner?" the guerilla leader spat. "These people are helping

our enemies." He leaned threateningly toward Bruce. "And maybe so are you." He shoved a small child into a mud puddle and pointed his gun at Bruce. The rest of the guerillas gathered around him, casting dangerous looks at Bruce.

"You shouldn't have done that," Bruce said calmly. "Now say you're sorry and get out of here."

The guerillas looked at one another and laughed.

"Why?" the leader asked, unmoved.

Of course the guerillas had no idea who or what they were facing. Not that they would have believed Bruce if he had told them. Still, Bruce wanted to be fair. "You're making me angry," Bruce warned. His eyes flashed and his muscles tightened, ready for the fight that was sure to come. "You wouldn't like me when I'm angry."